Listen With Your Third Ear.
The One In The Center Of Your Heart.

I0618288

A Scripture Parable Book
Series One: Book Two

CREATIVE
WORKS
PRESS

Leave Your Mark On The World.
Copyright 2020

ISBN: 978-1-951965-03-7 (Paperback)
Kindle Edition Available Through Amazon

Any references to historical events, real people, or real places are used fictitiously. Names, characters, and places are products of the author's imagination.

First Printed Edition 2020.

Creative Works Press
2001 Duncan Dr. NW Ste. #44
Kennesaw, GA 30156
404-307-9185
sales@creatorgraphics.com

www.CreativeWorks.cloud
www.CreatorGraphics.com

CREATIVE WORKS PRESS

Leave Your Mark On The World.

Liberty, The Little Birdie
(And The Cage That She Built)

A SCRIPTURE PARABLE BOOK
SERIES ONE: BOOK TWO

BY HEATH CHRISTOPHER GOODMAN
ILLUSTRATED BY YUFFIE YULIANA

Now, once upon a big blue sky lived a little birdie named Liberty.
On top of the clouds, Liberty flew to be close to Mr. Sunshine.
When she stayed near Him, she felt very safe and happy.

The presence of Mr. Sunshine made all high flying birds feel special.
He loved all the little birds and shined His joy on those near Him.
Every bird that flew above the clouds were friends of Mr. Sunshine.

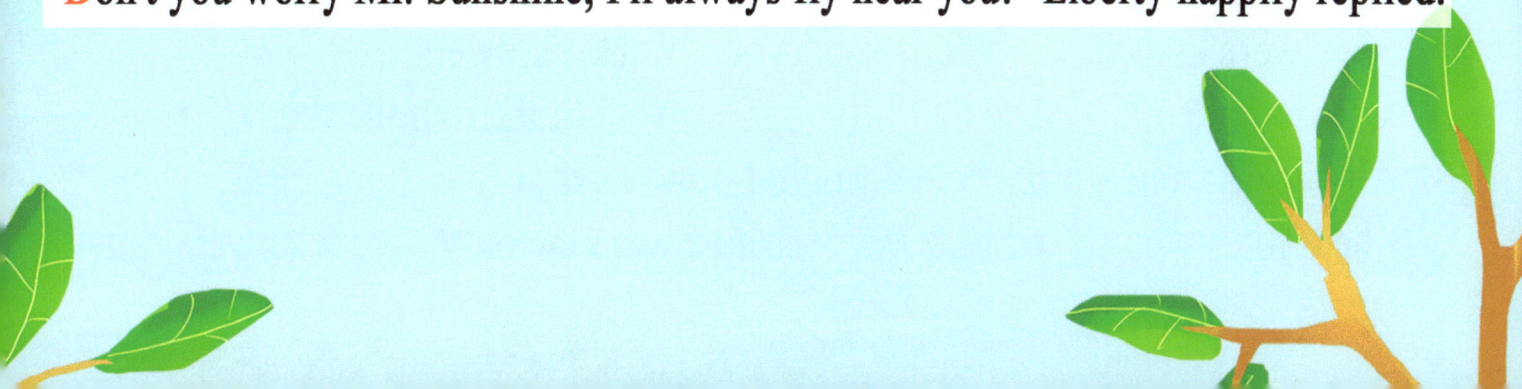

Liberty was very special to Mr. Sunshine for she was so innocent and free.
"Oh Liberty, do you know the meaning of your name?" Mr. Sunshine asked.
"Remember, you are meant to be free so stay close to me." Mr. Sunshine shined!
"Don't you worry Mr. Sunshine, I'll always fly near you!" Liberty happily replied.

It was known that angry birds lived on the ground who could no longer fly.
So many lived in cages and were part of "The Wounded Wings Club".

They were known as "Cage Dwellers" or "Rock Throwers".
How too often it seemed that little birdies would fall from the sky.
All because angry birds below would throw rocks at low flying birds.
The birdies who stayed near Mr. Sunshine were the only ones who were safe.

So Mr. Sunshine was always warning His flying friends to stay near Him.
Plenty of birdies had lost their way, flying too low and then crashed to the earth.
In the end, all angry birds on the ground were once happy birdies in the sky.
Rocks were thrown because angry birds were jealous of those who could fly.
It was a viscous cycle where birds who had been hurt wanted to hurt others too.
There soon became more angry birds and less happy ones with Mr. Sunshine.

After many birds had fallen, Mr. Sunshine grew very sad.
"No wounded bird ever seems to want to fly again!" He warned.
Day after day, the sky became lonelier and lonelier for Mr. Sunshine.

When birds didn't listen, they would always fall to the ground.
How Mr. Sunshine wished something could be done to save them all.
Early one morning, Liberty, the little birdie also flew way too low.
Rocks pelted her hard and she suddenly crashed to the earth below.
Every angry bird nearby mocked her and threw more rocks at her.

Trying to fly, Liberty finally gave up because her wings were broken.
Her heart sank as she remembered Mr. Sunshine's warnings.
"Every wounded bird seems to never be able to fly again."

Soon Liberty was forced to find a way to protect herself.
Powerless to fly, Liberty built her a cage like all the other angry birds.
It became the only safe place to keep from getting hurt.
Rocks could not touch her because of the cage's bars and walls.
In the end though, it also became Liberty's prison cell.
Through time she also began to forget all about Mr. Sunshine and His love.

Often Liberty would break down and cry, remembering when she could fly. Forgetting became easier though and soon Liberty just became bitter and angry.

Then Liberty began throwing rocks at other birds flying happily above her. Her heart was no longer innocent or free like it had been with Mr. Sunshine. Every flying bird was a painful reminder of crashing to the earth.

Liberty became a very angry bird locked in her cage with hatred.
One day Liberty threw rocks at a pure White Dove and hit him out of the sky.
Rocks were pelted at the White Dove by angry birds nearby.
Doves were rare birds and a pure white one was the rarest in all the world.

"I've been sent by Mr Sunshine to set you free!" shouted the White Dove.
"See, I am the very sunshine of Heaven come down in the form of a dove!"

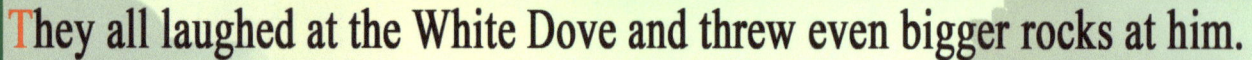

They all laughed at the White Dove and threw even bigger rocks at him.
Hurling her last stone, Liberty stepped out of her cage to get more rocks.
Except now all the angry birds near Liberty started hitting her with rocks as well.
Running back towards her cage, Liberty fell and passed out.
Escaping from the rocks, the White Dove bolted in front of Liberty to protect her.

Injured, the White Dove dragged Liberty inside her cage and then collapsed.
Soon Liberty awoke to find the White Dove laying completely still next to her.

Liberty realized the White Dove had saved her life.
It happened that the White Dove had died protecting Liberty from the rocks.
Bursting into tears, Liberty cried as she felt the weight of her shame and guilt.
Every angry bird near her scoffed at her for weeping.
Realizing how bitter she had become, Liberty whispered a prayer up to Heaven.
"To Mr. Sunshine, I am so sorry for killing the White Dove you sent to me."
"You loved me even while I was bitter and angry and yet I rejected your love."

It was just as Liberty finished praying when the White Dove became alive again.
From inside Liberty's cage, the White Dove's wings were completely healed.

The White Dove was now beautiful, radiant and happy.
He joyfully said, "Liberty, Mr. Sunshine forgives you and so do I!"
"Every stone you threw has been forgiven so come and fly with me, my friend!"

Suddenly fear, distrust and doubt filled Liberty's heart again.
"Oh how I wish I could trust you but this cage has protected me for so long."
"Neither can these wounded wings ever fly again." Liberty cried.

The White Dove replied, "Liberty, do you know the meaning of your name?"
"How you were always meant to be free, to fly with me, my dear friend!"
"Especially now that I have wings too!" said the White Dove winking at Liberty.
"Really, are you Mr. Sunshine with wings?" Liberty asked as hope rose up in her.
"Every bit of me is from Mr. Sunshine!" the White Dove said with a smile.

"For I am the Sonshine, the expressed image in the form of a pure white dove!"
"Only now I can help all the little birdies who have fallen to the earth!"
"Rocks have no power to hurt me" said the White Dove, spreading His wings.
Encircling Liberty's cage, the White Dove flew without getting wounded.

Soon angry birds threw more rocks but they only bounced off the White Dove.
Hurling the biggest stones, the White Dove hovered without even flinching.
"All the rocks in the world are no match for my love!" the White Dove sparkled.
"Leave your cages of bitterness, forgive and be forgiven to fly again!"
"Liberty, come now and fly with me!" shouted the White Dove.

Moments later, Liberty could hardly see the White Dove as He flew upward.
All at once Liberty went to the door of her cage.
"Keep inside your cage and you will be safe." She heard her fear say.
"Except I may never see the White Dove again." Liberty answered back.

Yelling from the clouds, the White Dove beckoned for Liberty to fly.
"Okay, I forgive those who hurt me so that I can be free again!" Liberty cried.
Up from the sky, a tear from Mr. Sunshine fell onto Liberty's broken wings!

Flooded with forgiveness, Liberty felt power as she lifted up her wings.
Rocks were immediately thrown at her but Liberty felt no pain or impact.
Empowered by the White Dove's love, Liberty flew up into the big blue sky!
Effortlessly, she flew over the clouds to Mr. Sunshine and the White Dove.

"You are Liberty and meant to be free!" Mr. Sunshine exclaimed.
"Oh, I am free from my cage and my bitterness!" Liberty beamed with joy.
Unshackled from all her distrust and fears, Liberty danced upon the clouds!

Sunshine and blue skies filled Liberty's eyes, her heart and her wings.

"How could have I have forgotten about you?" Liberty asked Mr. Sunshine.

"Anyone who lets the darkness in will push the light out." Mr. Sunshine replied.

"Liberty, will you help us show others they can be free?" asked the White Dove.

Liberty responded, "Of course, I will share this love that heals wounded wings!"

"But what if angry birds hurt me again?" Liberty asked with a tinge of doubt.
"Every hurt must be forgiven and is the secret to flying!" said the White Dove.

"Forgiveness is a lifetime of miracles, not just one!" Mr. Sunshine added.
"Rocks and dirt are certain to come from angry birds below."
"Even from angry birds close to you who are jealous of your freedom."
"Embrace their pain and your love will be invincible!" said the White Dove.

In and out of the clouds, Liberty playfully soared with the White Dove.
"Never again will you build a cage to imprison yourself!" Mr. Sunshine mused.
Diving below the clouds, Liberty felt forgiveness for all those who once hurt her.
Empowered with joy, she shared the love of the White Dove and Mr. Sunshine.
Eventually, many angry birds were healed and able to fly the big blue sky again.
Do you know the meaning of your name and how you were meant to be free?

THE BEGINNING!

"Now the Lord is that Spirit:
and where the Spirit of the Lord is, there is liberty." 2Corinthians 3:17
"If the Son therefore shall make you free, you shall be free indeed." John 8:36

Study The Word!

What did you learn from this scripture parable story?

Unfortunately, there is no way to travel through this life without getting hurt by someone or something. We must learn to be quick to forgive before a root of bitterness darkens our hearts. Only Jesus can give us this inner power. We might not be able to keep pain from entering our lives but we can be free from becoming bitter and angry through the love of God. To forgive someone doesn't mean you have to trust them. They must earn your trust but you can freely forgive them just as Christ forgave us.

Many people build cages where they live isolated, broken and embittered lives. They really think that their cage is their freedom and protection but it actually becomes their prison cell and their torture chamber.
They never realize that to love and to be loved is always going to make them vulnerable and susceptible to being hurt or abused. In this fallen world, loving others and being loved by others will always be a risky endeavor. However, the key to loving others and being loved is learning to forgive and be forgiven. If we could learn that letting go of the pain and hurt is far more easier than holding on to it and letting it fester as a chronic wound that never heals. God would have us all to be quick forgivers. This is the secret to true and lasting happiness.

Here are a few additional scriptures to study which support the concept of freedom through forgiveness-

"For if you forgive other people when they sin against you, your heavenly Father will also forgive you. But if you do not forgive others their sins, your Father will not forgive your sins." Matthew 6:14-15

"Forgive us our sins, for we also forgive everyone who sins against us. And lead us not into temptation." Luke 11:4

"Then Peter came to Jesus and asked, "Lord, how many times shall I forgive my brother or sister who sins against me? Up to seven times?" Jesus answered, "I tell you, not seven times, but seventy-seven times." Matthew 18:21-22

"Bear with each other and forgive one another if any of you has a grievance against someone. Forgive as the Lord forgave you." Colossians 3:13

"Be kind and compassionate to one another, forgiving each other, just as in Christ God forgave you." Ephesians 4:3

The Bible is full of instruction on how we should always seek to forgive or be forgiven of our sins. When we hold unforgiveness we are basically telling others that we are better than they are. Anyone of us can fall into sin and fall short of living how God wants us to live. We should learn to be quick to forgive just as we would want to be forgiven.

BOOKS FOR CHILDREN OF ALL AGES

Even more important than having an education in the subjects of math, science, history, etc., we need to give our children a moral foundation based on God's Precious Word. To neglect to guide our children, first by example and with lessons in Biblical morality is setting them up for moral ambiguity, confusion and ultimate failure in Godly living.

In today's world especially, if we don't take a stand against the evil tide rising, it is easy to get swept away by it through compromise and apostasy. As the scripture declares in *Isaiah 59:19*, *"...When the enemy shall come in like a flood, the Spirit of the LORD shall lift up a standard against him."*

This scripture parable is a great effort through much prayer in the Spirit to once again "raise up a holy standard" as the enemy tries to trample afoot our God fearing, Christian convictions and Biblical principles.

"Liberty, The Little Birdie" is part of a series of stories to teach Biblical morality and values in a fun and entertaining way to children of all ages. We hope you enjoy this second installment and will support our efforts by spreading the word about this book and the Scripture Parables series.

God bless you in the training of your children and remember God's precious promise to us-

"Train up a child in the way he should go: and when he is old, he will not depart from it."
Proverbs 22:6

Your Brother and Friend in Christ,
Heath Christopher Goodman

WE NEED CHRISTIAN AUTHORS WHO WANT TO RAISE UP A STANDARD OF HOLINESS IN THIS LAST HOUR!

Do you have a book inside you? Of course you do! Everyone of us has a story. Everyone of us has a lesson learned that could be turned into a story or teaching moment. We need Christian authors or "wanna-be authors" who want to inspire and touch the lives of others through their Christian writing. Leave your mark on the world. There is such a void in this world for God-fearing, morality based stories for our children and for adults. We need you to help raise up the standard of God's holiness! Whether it is fiction or nonfiction, a children's book or for us big kids, we want to help you edit, illustrate and publish or "self publish" your God inspired, "heart-on-fire" literary masterpiece! Contact us now!

Creative Works
2001 Duncan Dr. NW Ste. #44
Kennesaw, GA 30156
404-307-9185
sales@creatorgraphics.com
CreativeWorks.cloud
CreatorGraphics.com/book